The Big Race

a very t

Trevor Pye

Learning Media

Chapter 1

I remember the day I was picked to run in The Big Race. It felt like the worst day of my life. The worst day in the history of the universe! I felt very sorry for myself.

The race was for all the schools in our county. But my school, Duck Lake Elementary, was very small. There were only eleven students – and we weren't very good at sport.

Our principal, Mr. Springler, picked me out because I was tall. I had the longest legs in the school.

Other kids' legs

My legs

Duck Lake Elementary had never won
The Big Race. Every year when the
poster was put up, we all got the shivers.
Nobody wanted to be Duck Lake's
runner.

5

But every year, Mr. Springler picked someone to run in the race. "If you're not in, you can't win" was one of his favorite sayings.

And this year, the prize was extra special!

THE
BIG RACE

Inter-Schools
Annual Competition

BIG First Prize
6 Computers for
your school

Kindly donated by
Computers Unlimited Ltd.

I felt terrible. Our school was the worst in the history of the world at running. Everyone would be looking at me. But there was no way out! I even tried begging with Mr. Springler, but it was no use.

I would have to run with the whiz kids from the other schools. They were all faster than me. I could remember them well. Ben Banks, last year's winner. Milly McMinn, as strong as an ox. Otis Walker, with legs like an antelope ....

It was too terrible to think about!

Chapter 2

There was only a week to go until the race, and my body looked like a beanpole. I had to do some exercise.

So I tried really hard to get fit.
I ran.

I swam.

I lifted heavy things.

I even worked out
with Mom.

11

The kids at school tried to cheer me up …

… but that didn't work.
So I did some more exercise.

I did more press-ups.

I skipped.

I did one-armed chin-ups.

And I ate a lot of Dad's
special cereal.

At last, on the day before the race, I knew I was as fit as I could be. The problem was, I was *so* tired from all that exercise!

That night, I had to go to a "get-together" to meet the other runners.

And it *was* scary! There was Ben Banks and Milly McMinn and Otis Walker – and some other kids I didn't know.

When I got home, I couldn't get to sleep. I was scared I'd dream about the race.

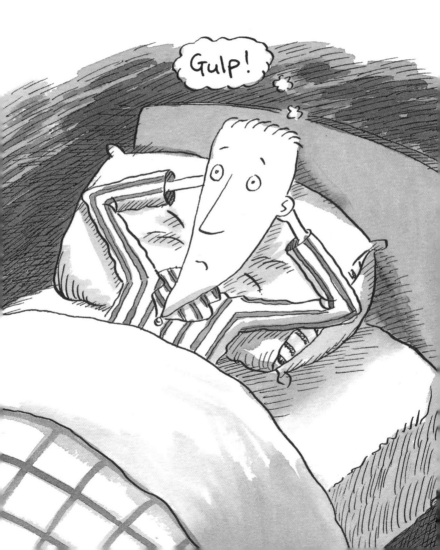

Next morning, I walked very slowly to school. Even my friend Richie couldn't cheer me up.

Mr. Springler was waiting at the school gates. He looked really happy. He really thought that I could win! That made me feel even worse.

Chapter 3

We all got into the school van. Mr. Springler drove to the sports field at the edge of town. That's where the race was going to start. I just stared out of the window. I had butterflies in my stomach, but the other kids were having a great time.

When we got to the field, Mr. Springler took me to a big tent.

I was weighed ...

and measured ...

and they gave me a life jacket.

what's this for?

Then they gave me the most important
thing – the map of the race.

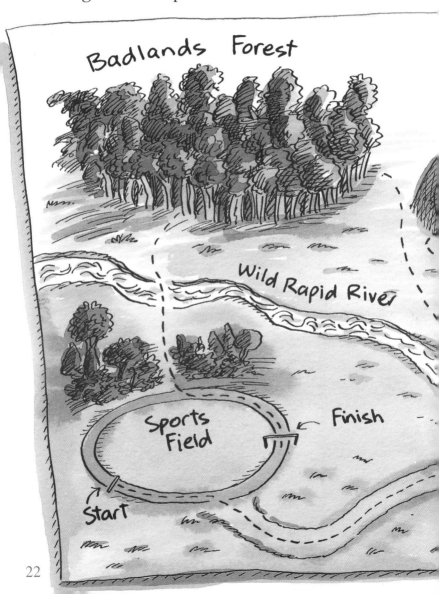

bald Eagle Mountains

Cliffs

Waterfall

Suddenly a loud voice came over the speaker. "All runners to the starting line, please." The Big Race was about to begin! I looked at the other nine runners. They all looked *super* fit.

The starter held up the gun and called –

Ten pairs of legs sprang into action.
Well, nine pairs, really. Mine "hopped"
into action.

We raced off the sports field and down a track. The track led to Wild Rapid River. So far, I was keeping up with the others. Maybe all my exercise had worked.

But Wild Rapid River was very fast.
Eight runners made it across. Then Dave
Dickens slipped. I grabbed his arm, but
we both floated away – along the river
and over a waterfall. Thank goodness for
the life jackets.

I swam to the shore at the bottom of the cliff. Dave Dickens was not so lucky. He floated out to sea. Luckily, a passing tanker picked him up.

When I got my breath back, I ran up the beach and saw the other runners. They were climbing down the cliffs.

Suddenly, a huge wave from the tanker crashed onto the beach. We were all knocked flat.

It was a terrible and frightening sight.

We were soaked to the skin, but nobody was hurt. Everyone jumped up and ran to the cliff. It looked *very* steep!

Up the cliff we went, and I was still with the others! When I got to the top, I checked my map. Then off I raced to the Bald Eagle Mountains.

When I got to Bald Eagle Mountains, the other runners had left me behind. I was puffed out, and my legs were sore.

As I ran into the mountains, I looked up. I could see big, black clouds, and large drops of rain started to fall. Everything was getting darker, *and* scarier.

Chapter 4

As I ran along the track, the rain got worse and worse. I think that was when the map fell out of my pocket.

Soon I came to a fork in the track, but the sign had been washed out by the rain. I felt for my map – it was gone!

There was only one thing left to do. I reached into my pocket and pulled out a quarter.

It was tails, so I took the right path. But it was the *wrong* path. Before long, I was lost – and still the rain poured down. I was just about to give up when I saw some shelter. It was an old mine.

I sat there in the old mine. It was dark and creepy, but it was out of the rain. As I sat watching the storm, I felt a cool breeze on my neck.

I ran through the cold, dark mine. It wasn't long before I saw light.

I walked out onto a rocky ledge. The sky was clear and bright. The storm had gone, but I didn't know where I was.

Suddenly, something swooped down on me. It was a very rare, giant bald eagle. It picked me up in its giant claws and flew off into the sky.

The other runners were having problems as well. One of the other runners had been picked up by a giant bald eagle too. It carried him to its nest, high in the mountains.

Milly McMinn and Ben Banks got as far as the Badlands Forest. Then they were chased up a tree by Badlands Forest wolves!

Good dog. Good dog.

The others had all made it through the Bald Eagle Mountains and the Badlands Forest. They were just going to cross the Wild Rapid River for the last time.

I was not so lucky. When I opened my eyes and looked down, I could see the ground – hundreds of feet below.

I screamed and fainted. I must have given the eagle a shock because it dropped me.

Luckily, I landed in some thick, soft bushes. I got up and wobbled toward the finish line. But Otis Walker was right behind me. He ran like the wind.

Mr. Springler and the kids from Duck Lake cheered. They couldn't believe their eyes. Just as Otis was going to pass me, I tripped and fell ...

... over the finish line.

I beat Otis by a nose! Mr. Springler and the kids went wild. For the first time ever, Duck Lake Elementary had won The Big Race.

I didn't know I had won the race. I was lying across the finish line, exhausted and fast asleep.

That's how I remember the day I won The Big Race. I'm *sure* that's just how it happened.